Fart M

The Hilarious Misadventures of Jimmy Smith

Book # 1

Written & Illustrated By:
Mark Smith

ISBN-13: 978-1493510191

ISBN-10: 1493510193

Table of Contents

My Fart Monster

Shhhhh! Can you keep a secret? My name is Jimmy Smith, and I have something to tell you.

The old monster under the bed is nothing new. Every kid in the world knows that monsters live under their beds. It is a common fact. I mean, they have even made movies about this, but the monster that lives under my bed is a little different. He is not big and scary. He is not mean and hairy. He does not drool and he does not have sharp teeth. My monster, yes I call him mine. My monster makes me laugh. Do you know why he makes me laugh?

He makes me laugh because he is gassy. He has the thunder from down under. He has a booming butt. To put it simply, he is a farting monster. Just like you and I breathe, this guy cuts the cheese, and these are not some little butt burps either. These things are full blown earth shakers. This monster really knows how to rip one, and the worst part about it is, I always get the blame for it. What can you do? I can't really complain about it to my parents. Just imagine how that would play out.

Mom and Dad Meet My Stinky Little Friend

"Mom, Dad. I have something to tell you. A monster lives under my bed. This is no ordinary monster either."

My dad would probably ask me, "Does he have big eyes and bad breath?" He would stretch his face out by pulling the skin around his eyes trying to do his best monster impression. My mom on the other hand would say something like this. "Oh Jimmy, I told you not to watch those silly monster movies all the time."
"Mom, Dad, I am serious. There is a monster that is living under my bed. Come here, let me show you."

Right now that little monster is waiting under my bed. He has been listening to my whole conversation. Hey, monsters have super hearing you know.

While he has been listening, he has been brewing up one of the worst cases of gas this side of the border. He is ready to make the paint peel from the walls. He has some serious pucker power, and he is ready to show my mom and dad what he is made of. I can just see it now.

Mom and Dad Get A Big Stinky Surprise

My mom and dad enter my bedroom. They are good parents, so they are entertaining the idea of a monster living under my bed. My dad will want to prove to me that I am wrong while my mom and him look under the bed with a flashlight, but boy are they going to get butt blasted.

I try to stop them, but like all parents, they are very persistent. What is it with parents and persistence anyways? They just don't seem to stop.

They both get on their hands and knees and stick their heads under the bed. This is not going to be good.
As soon as the flashlight flicks on, a small explosion goes off under the bed. I see my mom and dad's bodies flinch. Then I hear my mom start to scream. Wait a minute, that is not my mom. That is my dad.

My mom is speechless, but her new hairdo that has been caused by the butt blast looks good. Her right eye starts to twitch as she begins to understand what just happened to her. Meanwhile, my dad is still screaming like a little girl. He never knew what hit him. Yeah, I don't think it would be a very good idea to tell my parents about the farting monster that lives under my bed.

What Do You Do With A Fart Monster?

So what is a kid like me supposed to do with a farting monster? I could think of at least a hundred things to do with this little guy, but I won't bore you with all of them. Aw, who am I kidding? Let's explore the possibilities!

Idea #1
I could take the fart monster to school with me. Just imagine how much fun that would be. All the teachers and bullies would never knew what hit them.

Idea #2

I could take the fart monster to the library and let him fill the library with wonderful sounds and smells. The library would never be the same again.

Idea #3

I could introduce my fart monster to my best friend Chuck. Chuck and the fart monster could compare stink bombs. The two of them together would be a toxic duo!

Idea #4

I could use the power of the fart monster to get out of school. If my parents caught a whiff of the gas that this guy created, they would definitely think I was sick.

Idea #5

I could use the fart monster to get revenge on my evil sister. That sounds perfect.

I think it is time to introduce my little friend to my sister.

My Evil Sister

I was lucky enough to only have one sister. She was far from an angel. To say that she picked on me would be a nice way of putting it. In fact, her favorite thing to do was literally pick and flick on me. Do you know where I am going with this?

Girls are supposed to be, well...um...girly and dainty like a flower, right? Wrong! This is just some disguise that girls have been practicing for years. I still think that moms must secretly teach their daughters how to be nice and all smiles one minute, and booger flicking monsters the next.

That's right, my sister was a picker, and a grinner and a flicker. She had this combination down better than you could ever imagine. If there was an Olympic booger flicking competition, she would win the gold medal for sure! Can you guess who her target always was? Yep. It was me.

She would mutter under her breath, "Whatcha doing booger boy?"

That was always the prelude to booger madness. Within seconds a gnarly brown booger would be airborne. No matter where I went, the booger always found me. It had some type of radar system that the Pentagon would be proud of. It may be a direct hit right under the eye, or it may lodge itself in my hair. Either way I was doomed.

Who has brown boogers anyways? That's not normal. There was something wrong with my sister. Deep down inside, I knew this. I could tell just by that evil look in her eye. The brown boogers were just the proof that my sister was from another world, and I am trying to be nice here. After a lifetime of being her little booger target, I could not wait to introduce her to my little farting monster. It would be a literal blast.

My Fart Filled Plan for Revenge

If I was going to pull this off, if I was going to teach my booger flicking older sister a lesson, then I had to be very smart about it. I had to devise a master plan of sorts. I would need to put some thought into this. I scratched my head, squinted my eyes and the perfect plan slowly started to take shape in my mind.

My sister always spent too much time in the bathroom "getting ready", and on Friday nights it was even worse. This Friday night she had a big date. She had been talking about it now for what seemed like months. Who in their right mind would want to date my evil sister? The guy would have to be nuts.

She would need extra time to get ready for her big date. That would give me the perfect opportunity to get my sister back for all those booger flicking years. If I played my cards right, she would never flick another booger at me as long as she lived.

The Secret Fart Equation

The first part of my plan meant that I had to load my little fart monster up with some really nasty fart brewing food. What types of foods make the nastiest farts?

I know broccoli is way up there on the list of best fart fuels, but I did not want to torture my little monster by making him eat healthy veggies. There had to be something else that would work.

Spicy foods always seem to help my dad brew up a batch of eye watering farts. When he eats spicy food, he practically paints the walls with his farts. The fog that comes from his butt is so thick, you will need a gas mask to survive. That would be too much. I new exactly what I needed, my mom's egg salad. Hey, that reminds me of a joke.

What did the egg salad sandwich say to the peanut butter and jelly sandwich?

Nothing. It just farted!

This stuff was gross. I mean, come on. Egg and salad should never be in the same sentence let alone some goofy food concoction. Our house turned an awful shade of green when my mom started making this stuff. Even the plants in the house wilted from the toxic fumes.

I had to do whatever it took to get some of my mom's vicious egg salad. I had to start priming this little fart monster. Getting the egg salad would be easy, or so I thought.

Egg Salad Farts

Have you ever been walking through a store, and suddenly you pass through a foreign fart zone? Someone in the store has let loose some seriously gross blue cheese farts so thick that they almost transport you to another dimension when you walk through the cloud. You have to stop for a second to recover from the nasal assault that has just happened.

Your brain does not know how to handle these situations. In some cases, it may even start to shut down. The best thing for you to do is get out of the store and get some fresh air.

This is what my mom's egg salad smelled like, and if it smelled this bad going in, you could only imagine how bad it was coming out. I am talking full on apocalyptic farts of doom. White vans, hazmat suits and gas masks would be needed in order to survive the methane that this stuff produced. I stayed away from it. I don't know how my dad could eat it, but he always did, and we all suffered from it.

My Dad Is the Fart Master

I think my dad enjoyed being the only one who could tolerate this fart brewing food. He always ate it knowing what would happen. It was all part of his diabolical payback plan. Come on. You know what I am talking about.

Any guy that says his dad has not lifted off the ground from what could only be a rocket fueled fart is not telling the truth. Just like moms are secretly teaching their daughters how to be nice and smiles one minute and booger flicking monsters the next, dads are teaching their sons the art of the fart.

My dad would pinch off some squeakers that sounded like someone was letting the air out of a balloon. My dad had what he proudly proclaimed as, "Sphincter control!" This was a hereditary trait that had been passed down for generations, and my dad told me that I would soon have this awesome power.

I didn't know if I wanted this self proclaimed power. Why couldn't the male family trait be something like chiseled looks or six pack abs? I get stuck with "Sphincter control." Oh joy.

Sometimes my dad would silently fart dust the entire family, and then decide that it was time to go for a walk. One mention of egg salad, and my dad was smiling from ear to ear. This was the perfect fuel for my little fart brewing buddy.

Friday Will Be Fartacular!

Fartacular? Is that even a word? It is now. When your friends try to tell you that fartacular is not a word. You tell them it is, and you can prove it to them. When they ask how, just pinch off your best ripper and exclaim, "That was fartacular!"

I would start putting my plan into action early Friday afternoon. This would give my fart monster plenty of time to sit and brew. When Friday night arrived, I would be transformed into an artist. My sister would be my canvas and my medium would be pure fart. I was going to be painting it on really thick.

Friday could not come soon enough. It was times like this that I wish I had a time machine. I could just push a few buttons and be magically transported to that special moment when I would finally get my revenge.

Fart Monster Wake Up Call

What kind of alarm clock do you use? For a lot of my friends, their morning wake up call comes in the form of a screaming mom! I have seen my friend's moms and I would not want them waking me up every morning. That would be a nightmare for sure.

There are some kids that have a normal alarm clock. I have one of those too, but ever since my fart monster appeared, he has been waking me up every morning with his butt thunder. My whole bed shakes, and then the smell slowly rises covering my entire body like a warm blanket.

There are some kids that have a normal alarm clock. I have one of those too, but ever since my fart monster appeared, he has been waking me up every morning with his butt thunder. My whole bed shakes, and then the smell slowly rises covering my entire body like a warm blanket.

This is my morning wake up call. Care to trade with me?

No Fart Fuel

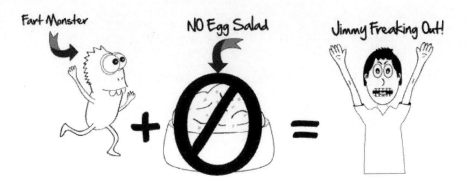

All I had to do was go downstairs, fill a bowl with the egg salad and carry it to my room. That is it. Is that asking too much? Is it? No it is not, but unfortunately for me things did not work out like that. Can you guess what happened?

As sure as the sun will rise and set every single day, my mother will make her egg salad every Thursday night, but apparently the one time that I needed this nasty stuff, she decided not to make it. There must have been some weird planetary alignment that was not working in my favor.

Panic started to set in. How in the world was I going to go through with my plan if I did not have the fuel to feed that little stink bomb upstairs. Sure, he was smelly enough on his own, but I had to unleash a stink unlike any other if I was going to get my sister back for all those years of booger torture. This could only mean one thing.

Mom I Need Fart Fuel

"Mom?" I said with a huge smile on my face.

"Where is the egg salad?"

A silence fell over the kitchen. My dad looked up from his cup of brown goo that he called coffee. My sister stopped crunching on her bowl of choco nuggets. The corners of her mouth were covered in little black crumbs. I could only imagine how bad her breath must have smelled.

The room was so quiet that I could hear my heart beating in my chest. I was now the center of attention, and I had to be calm and cool.

Here is the problem. My family knows that I don't like egg salad so by asking this simple question, I threw everything off. It was as if time stood still for what seemed like 10-15 seconds.

"What did you say honey?" asked my mom.

I kept smiling and said, "Where is the egg salad?"

My mom's eye brows got all squished as she stared at me. I could see the gears in her head moving. She knew what I had just asked her, but to her it just wasn't making any sense.

Fart Fuel Success

"Egg salad?" my mom asked. "Why do you want my egg salad?" My mom wasn't buying it. She knew I was up to something. How is it that moms always seem to know?

I just kept smiling and said, "I thought it would be good for lunch."

My mom's face changed again. This time it looked as if someone had just slapped her. All of the emotion drained from her face. Her eye brows were no longer squished. I glanced over at my dad. His face changed too. His mouth formed a huge smile. He was proud of me.

"The boy is growing up honey!" my dad said proudly. "His tastes are changing."

This was all my mom needed to snap her out of it. With the encouragement of my dad, she was now starting to change as well. The color was coming back to her face. A smile slowly formed on her lips.

Was my dad really on my side, or was he just happy to make me eat some of that nasty egg salad? I started to doubt his enthusiasm. Maybe he was really just trying to poison me with this stuff. Nah. My dad was happy. I could see it in his eyes. He was glad to have someone else on his side. He was probably thinking that the two of us could fart dust the family with nasty egg salad farts at the same time. It looked like my plan was working perfectly, except for one thing. Now I would be stuck with an egg salad sandwich for lunch.

Fart Revenge Clouds the Mind

It was hard to focus on anything that day in school. My mind was busy thinking about getting revenge on my sister.

The final class bell rang, and I ran the entire way home. I still had the egg salad sandwich in my backpack. There was no way that I was going to eat that nasty thing. Plus, the longer I let this methane brewing bomb sit, the more powerful my little fart monster was going to be. This was going to be a literal blast!

I bet the egg salad left a nasty green trail of stink behind me as I ran down the sidewalk. All of the kids who were behind me must have thought I was farting up a storm, or that I had pooped my pants. I didn't care one bit. My plan was about to be completed. I laughed like a mad scientist who has just created a monster.

Feeding the Fart Monster

When I got home, I ran right to my room. When I opened my bedroom door, the smell slapped me across the face. If you were standing right next to me at this moment you might say, "Gee Jimmy, why are you crying?" But these were not tears. It was a natural self defense my body conjured up to protect my eyes from all the stink. My little fart monster had been letting them rip all day. The toxic green cloud that filled my room was living proof.

I pulled the egg salad sandwich from my backpack and tossed it under the bed. My room fell silent. I watched my bed closely for some magical sign that my plan was working. The bed shifted a little. Then it started to shake. It suddenly looked as if it were possessed by a crazed demon. It lifted off the floor, spun around in circles and came crashing to the floor with a loud bang. My room was silent again. Was the egg salad too much for the little guy? Did I just poison my fart monster?

The room started to shake from what could only be the loudest fart/burp that I have ever heard. This thing would have made an elephant proud. If this was any indication of what my sister was in for, then she may need to buy a wig after I let the monster loose in the bathroom because I think that burp/fart just caused all of my hair to wither away and fall out. It was the most brutal fart that I have ever experienced. This put my Dad's farting skills to shame!

Time For Revenge!

Like clockwork, my sister started getting ready for her big date four hours ahead of time. She spent about two hours of it on the phone gossiping with her friends. They talked about boring girl stuff like: which outfit she should wear, what shoes would look the best and whether she should put her hair up or wear it down.

Bla bla blabity bla. It was enough to make you want to puke. The wait was killing me. How could she talk on the phone for such a long time? Hang up the phone already!

Time For Revenge!

I finally heard her leave her room and head for the bathroom. Everything was working perfectly. I had already stashed the fart monster under the bathroom sink. All I had to do was feed the monster some of that nasty egg salad, and wait for the rest of my plan to fall perfectly into place.

Chocolate Chip Egg Salad Cookies

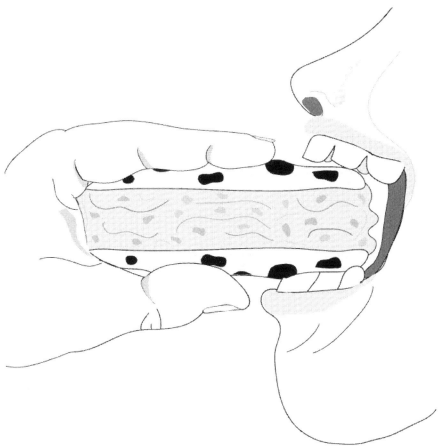

I ran downstairs and opened the refrigerator. Where was the egg salad? I couldn't see it anywhere. Oh no! I started to panic, and that is when I heard my Dad say, "Whatcha looking for son?"

There he was sitting at the kitchen table. Can you guess what he had? If you guessed the chocolate chip cookies, you were partly right. He had those and he had the bowl of egg salad too. He was making egg salad sandwiches, but he was not using bread. He was using chocolate chip cookies instead.

As if listening to my sister's girl talk on the phone was not enough to make me puke, this just might do it. My dad had sunk to an all time low. He was making chocolate chip cookie egg salad sandwiches. This was beyond gross and I could only imagine how we would all suffer later tonight when his crazy snack food decided to emerge from his butt.

I smiled and said, "That looks great dad! Can I have one?"

My dad didn't even think twice about it. He threw one chocolate chip cookie down on the table, spooned a heaping helping of egg salad on top of it and squished the entire mess together with another chocolate chip cookie on top. The egg salad oozed from the sides.

"Thanks dad! I will eat this in my room if you don't mind."

My dad never even looked up from his snack.

Sneaking Into the Bathroom

It was time to put my years of watching spy movies and playing stealthy video games to work. There was no way my sister was going to take a shower without locking the bathroom door. Not only would I have to unlock the door, but I would have to sneak in the bathroom without being heard. It was time to become a ninja.

I grabbed my ninja costume from the closet and slipped it on. What? You don't have a ninja costume in your closet? Everyone should have a ninja costume in their closet. You never know when you may need it.

I silently walked down the hall towards the bathroom. I could hear the shower running. I placed my hand on the bathroom door knob and slowly turned it. My sister forgot to lock the door! I couldn't believe my luck.

I was in the bathroom and I could see my sister's silhouette through the shower curtain. She was singing, but her singing suddenly stopped. Something was wrong. I could see her reaching for the shower curtain. I had to do something quick.

Dad's Dirty Underwear

There was only one place to hide. I did my best ninja move and ended up in the dirty clothes hamper. I could see what was going on through the holes in the side of the basket. My sister stuck her head out of the shower and looked around. Whew! I was safe for the time being.

I slowly exhaled and took a deep breath. That's when it hit me. The clothes hamper was full of my dad's dirty clothes and a pair of his underwear was now covering my left eye. One of his dirty socks managed to land right on my nose. My smile quickly turned into a frown. What would you do in this situation?

At this point I started to doubt my plan. It looked as if little mister ninja boy was the one getting the worst part of the deal. I bet this never happened to other ninjas.

Wait a minute. My dad's underwear was covering my left eye. That meant that the.... I panicked and jumped out of the dirty clothes hamper.

My sister was already back in the shower and singing again. Time to feed the fart monster.

The Final Feeding

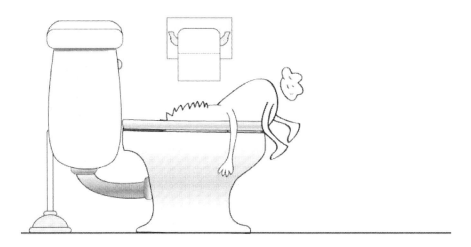

That was a really close call. I looked in the mirror and realized that I still had my dad's dirty underwear hanging from my head. I shook my head and the underwear fell to the floor.

I opened the cabinets under the bathroom sink, but I couldn't see the fart monster anywhere. What else could possibly go wrong? He was nowhere to be found.

I turned around and scanned the bathroom. The little guy was standing on the edge of the toilet with his head in the bowl. Was he doing what I thought he was doing? Yep. He was drinking from the toilet.

I waved the egg salad cookie sandwich in the air. The little fart monster got a whiff of it and jumped off the toilet. I threw the cookie sandwich under the bathroom sink, and the fart monster eagerly followed. I slowly closed the cabinet door and quietly made my exit.

Revenge Is Stinky Sweet

I didn't have much time until the fart bomb went off. I quickly grabbed a chair and stuck it under the handle of the bathroom door. The door opened out, and this would prevent my sister from escaping once the smell started to creep into the shower.

T-Minus 10 seconds and counting. This had to be the longest ten seconds of my life. 10...9...8...7...6...5...

At the five second mark I started to doubt everything. Was I doing the right thing? Was all of this going to be too much for my poor sister to handle?

I started to remember all the good times we have had in the past. I saw her smiling face as we exchanged gifts on Christmas morning. I saw her smiling face at her last birthday party when she shared her last piece of birthday cake with me.

Then I saw her smiling face transform into that evil grin that always showed up when she flicked boogers at me. I was 100% positive that I was doing the right thing. My sister was long overdue.

Then I saw her smiling face transform into that evil grin that always showed up when she flicked boogers at me. I was 100% positive that I was doing the right thing. My sister was long overdue.

There was a thump at the door as my sister tried to escape, but she was trapped. She pounded on the door.

"Who is it?" I said.

"JIMMY!!!! OPEN THIS DOOR RIGHT NOW!" screamed my sister.

"Say pleeeasssee!" I said.

"JIMMY. I AM NOT KIDDING AROUND WITH YOU. LET ME OUT OF HERE!" my sister screamed.

"You didn't say the magic word," I said.

"PLEASE JIMMY!" she yelled.

I opened the door and my sister ran out of the bathroom. The disgusting green egg salad gas the fart monster created stuck to my sister like a second skin as she ran down the hall. I couldn't help but laugh. They say revenge can be sweet, but in this case it was stinky sweet!

Huge Farting Success!

My plan for revenge was a huge success. My sister never knew what happened! I wasn't done with the fart monster yet. I still had a few great ideas where he would come in really handy.

I think it was time to get revenge on the meanest bully that ever lived. His name was Fred. It didn't take much to conjure up an image of Fred in my mind.

He was the meanest, he was the weirdest and he was the biggest kid in eighth grade. If that was not enough to make you poop you pants, then one look into his eyes would make any kid tremble with fear.

Fred's eyes were two different colors. His left eye was blue and his right eye was brown. I know this because Fred has been bullying me since the 2nd grade. Yep, it was time for some more stinky sweet revenge!

Will Jimmy's plan for revenge be a success, or will Fred continue his reign of bullying terror?

Get your own copy of Bye Bye Bully Book # 2 in the series and find out for yourself!

Printed in Great Britain
by Amazon